Happy holidays!

-J.G.

ISBN: 978-1-7346367-5-8

# Duncan and Daisy's
# North Pole Adventure

By Joy Garcia

Duncan and Daisy had one Christmas wish this year; to visit Santa at the North Pole.

Duncan said doubtfully, "Gee Daisy, do you really think we'll be able to meet Santa?"

"Yes, I do and we're going to see him at the North Pole," said Daisy with great faith.

They got their pens and paper out and started to write:

Dear Santa,

We really, really, really want to go see you at the North Pole for our Christmas present. We've been very good this year.

Love,
Duncan and Daisy

On Christmas Eve morning, Duncan and Daisy heard a knock on their front door. When they opened the door, they found a letter and a large package.

Duncan was in shock and in disbelief when he looked at the letter, "Daisy look! It's a letter from Santa!"

"Hurry let's read it!" shouted Daisy.

To: Duncan and Daisy

From: Santa

Dear Duncan and Daisy,

　　You two have been such good little dogs. I am granting your wish by inviting you to the North Pole to come see me. I've sent you both a magic sleigh that is powered by Christmas spirit. I've also sent special hats, mittens, and scarves to keep you extra warm.

Sincerely,
Santa

Duncan and Daisy thought this was all a dream as they hopped onto the magical sleigh. The sleigh took them up North and when they finally arrived at the North Pole, some big majestic polar bears came out to greet them.

"Hi Mrs. Polar Bear. Do you know where Santa is?" asked Duncan.

"Hello," said Mrs. Polar Bear. "We just saw him at Gingerbread Lane. If you like, we can show you the way."

"Oh yes, that would be nice!" said Duncan.

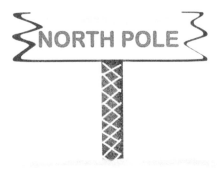

When they all arrived at Gingerbread Lane, the polar bears said their goodbyes and went back home.

Duncan and Daisy looked all around for Santa. They saw a house made out of gingerbread, gumdrops, lollipops, and all different kinds of yummy candy, but no Santa. Then they saw Mr. and Mrs. Gingerbread.

"Hi, have you seen Santa?" asked Daisy.

"Hi," replied Mrs. Gingerbread. "We saw him at Hot Chocolate River earlier. He might still be there. Would you like us to bring you there?"

"That would be great!" said Daisy.

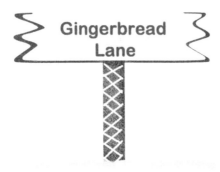

Mr. and Mrs. Gingerbread showed them the way. They wished Duncan and Daisy good luck and went back home.

The sweet smell of chocolate filled the air at Hot Chocolate River. The little dogs took the sleigh down the dark chocolate waterfall and onto the river. As they floated along, they saw marshmallows, huge chocolate chip cookies, peppermint sticks, whipped cream, and more. All these sweet treats in sight, but no Santa!

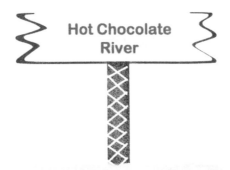

Duncan and Daisy exited the river and came to a stop at Frosty Igloo. There were snowmen that twisted and twirled on ice as the fluffy snowflakes fell gently through the sky.

"Hi Snowman family, have you seen Santa?" asked Duncan.

"Hello," said Mr. Snowman. "He was just here a few moments ago. He said he had to talk to the reindeer about tonight's Christmas delivery. We can show you where to go, if you like."

"Yes please," Duncan replied gratefully.

They arrived at a place named Reindeer Landing. The Snowman family waved goodbye and went back to their Igloo.

Duncan and Daisy looked around and didn't see anyone on the ground. Then they looked up and saw streaks of glittery sparkles in the atmosphere. It was the reindeer shooting across the sky. Duncan and Daisy flew up towards the reindeer.

Daisy said to one of the reindeer, "Hi. Have you seen Santa?"

"Hi," said the reindeer with a red nose. "Yes, he just left on his sleigh. We're going to meet him later at the Grand Ole Christmas Tree. Follow us and we'll take you there."

"Thank you so much!" Daisy said with glee.

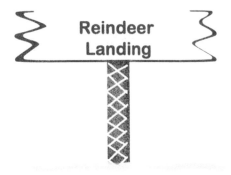

They all swooped down towards the Grand Ole Christmas Tree. The tree glowed so bright they could see it from up in the air. When they all landed, the reindeer said bye and went back up into the sky to practice for their big Christmas night delivery.

As Duncan and Daisy waited, they noticed how small they were compared to the huge Christmas tree. It was the biggest one they had ever seen. The dogs waited and waited some more for Santa, but Santa was nowhere in sight!

They sat in silence, not sure what to do. Then ever so quietly they heard little voices singing nearby.

"Fa, la, la…"

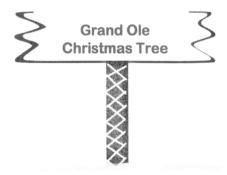

Duncan and Daisy followed the sound and were surprised to find Christmas elves singing so cheerfully as they packed Christmas presents into a huge, red velvety bag with golden ropes.

Duncan and Daisy said to the elves, "Hi, do you know where Santa is?"

"Hi," said one of the elves. "Santa is at his house right down this hill. He's getting ready for his Christmas delivery. Would you like us to take you there?"

"Thank you, but we see that you are busy. We can find it!" Duncan and Daisy said confidently.

The elves pointed the way and wished them joy and happiness.

Duncan and Daisy thought, "Surely this is it, the moment we will finally get to see Santa!".

They zoomed down the hill as fast as they could, but then a heavy blanket of white snow started to fall. The snow was so thick that they couldn't see where to go.

Duncan started to lose hope, "Oh no, we're never going to see Santa! We'll be stuck here all day!"

"Don't worry Duncan we'll make it. We just have to believe we can," Daisy said so hopefully. "Say it with me Duncan…"

"WE CAN, WE CAN, WE CAN!" they chanted together.

Duncan and Daisy's Christmas spirit caused the magical sleigh to get stronger and the sleigh was able to speed up and move past the snow storm with ease.

Then, suddenly, they heard a booming voice that shook the ground.

"HO, HO, HO!"

Duncan and Daisy looked around and to their delight they saw a great big man with a red fluffy suit sitting in a chair just a few yards away.

"SANTA!" exclaimed Duncan and Daisy. "We've been trying to find you all day!"

Santa said, "Ah, you see, that was my plan all along. I invited you here to not just see me, but to make new friends and to have a North Pole adventure to remember. You've also shown great hope even when things got tough and that is the greatest gift of all; to have hope, faith, and perseverance."

Duncan and Daisy felt so proud. They really did do all those things.

And with that, Santa gave them a hug and wished them a very happy Christmas.

When it was time for Duncan and Daisy to return home, they hopped in the sleigh and waved goodbye to Santa and to all their new friends.

Their Christmas wish had been fulfilled and it was the very best Christmas they ever had. As for Duncan, he was so glad to have a friend like Daisy who was there to help him believe.

The end.

Dear Santa,

"What do you wish for?"

# Meet the real Duncan and Daisy!

sweet girl

Lightning Source UK Ltd.
Milton Keynes UK
UKHW021522171220
375250UK00002B/7